Note to parents, carers and teachers

Read it yourself is a series of modern stories, favourite characters, traditional tales and first reference books, written in a simple way for children who are learning to read. The books can be read independently or as part of a guided reading session.

Each book is carefully structured to include many high-frequency words vital for first reading. The sentences on each page are supported closely by pictures to help with understanding, and to offer lively details to talk about.

The books are graded into four levels that progressively introduce wider vocabulary and longer text as a reader's ability and confidence grows.

Ideas for use

- Although your child will now be progressing towards silent, independent reading, let her know that your help and encouragement is always available.

- Developing readers can be concentrating so hard on the words that they sometimes don't fully grasp the meaning of what they're reading. Answering the quiz questions at the end of the book will help with understanding.

For more information and advice on Read it yourself and book banding, visit www.ladybird.com/readityourself

Book Band 10

Level 4 is ideal for children who are ready to read longer stories with a wider vocabulary and are eager to start reading independently.

Special features:

Richer, more varied vocabulary

Full, exciting story

Detailed illustrations capture the imagination

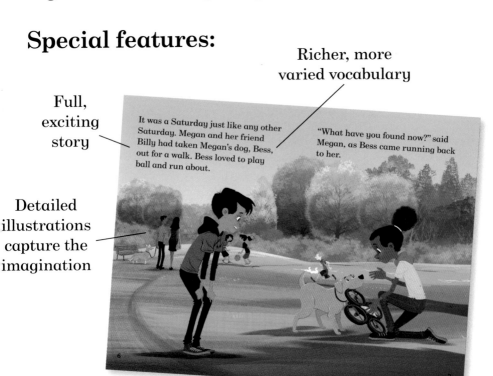

It was a Saturday just like any other Saturday. Megan and her friend Billy had taken Megan's dog, Bess, out for a walk. Bess loved to play ball and run about.

"What have you found now?" said Megan, as Bess came running back to her.

6

7

Longer sentences

Clear type

Dad put the movie from the drone's camera on his laptop.

He played the movie. He, Megan and Billy all watched.

The first thing they saw was a boy's face, looking up at them.

"That's Shivam, isn't it Billy?" said Megan. Shivam was one of their friends.

21

Educational Consultant: Geraldine Taylor
Book Banding Consultant: Kate Ruttle

LADYBIRD BOOKS

UK | USA | Canada | Ireland | Australia
India | New Zealand | South Africa

Ladybird Books is part of the Penguin Random House group of companies
whose addresses can be found at global.penguinrandomhouse.com.

www.penguin.co.uk   www.puffin.co.uk   www.ladybird.co.uk

First published 2017
This edition 2019
001

Copyright © Ladybird Books Ltd, 2017

Printed in China

ISBN: 978-0-241-40540-6

All correspondence to:
Ladybird Books
Penguin Random House Children's
80 Strand, London WC2R 0RL

The Mystery Drone

Written by Richard Dungworth
Illustrated by Amit Tayal

It was a Saturday just like any other Saturday. Megan and her friend Billy had taken Megan's dog, Bess, out for a walk. Bess loved to play ball and run about.

"What have you found now?" said
Megan, as Bess came running back
to her.

"It's a drone!" said Billy.

"A what?" said Megan.

"You know!" said Billy. "You fly them. They're cool! You must have seen one before. Loads of my friends have them."

Megan took a good look at the drone.

"Look!" she said, suddenly. "There's something written on the back. It's a message!"

"What does it say?" said Billy.

Megan showed him the message.

It just said "HELP!"

"Help?" said Billy. "Help who? And where are they?"

"I've no idea," said Megan. "It's a mystery!"

Billy looked at the message again.

"What do you think we should do?" he said.

"We should show my dad," said Megan. "He'll know what to do!"

Bess barked as if to say, "That's a good idea!"

They hurried back to Megan's house to show her dad what they had found.

Dad had a good look at the drone and the message written on it.

"There must be some way to find out where it came from," he said.

"I think I've got it!" said Billy, suddenly.

He had just seen that the drone had a camera.

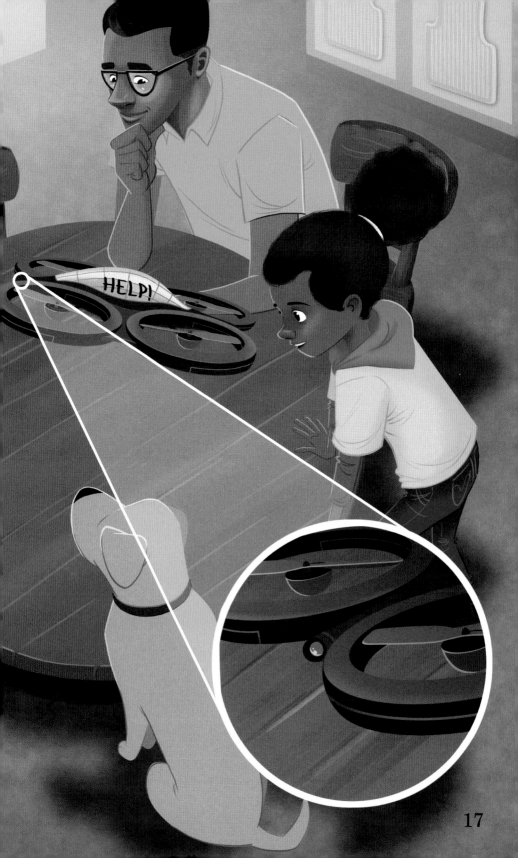

"When you fly a drone like this one, its camera takes a movie," said Billy. "So if we watch the movie . . ."

". . . We can see which way the drone went!" said Megan. "And where it came from!"

"Good thinking!" said Dad. "I'll get my laptop."

Dad put the movie from the drone's camera on his laptop.

He played the movie. He, Megan and Billy all watched.

The first thing they saw was a boy's face, looking up at them.

"That's Shivam, isn't it, Billy?" said Megan. Shivam was one of their friends.

The movie played on. Billy saw trees and water, from above.

"Is that the river?" he said. "Things look funny from so high up!"

"There's the old bridge," said Dad.
"Do you see?"

"Yes," said Megan, "I see it!"

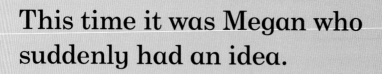

This time it was Megan who suddenly had an idea.

"We can match the movie to a map," she said. "Maps on the internet show things from above, too."

"Cool idea, Meg!" said Billy.

Dad got out his phone. They watched the drone movie again.

This time they matched what they saw in the movie to the internet map on Dad's phone.

"It looks like it took off near the Potts' farm," said Dad.

They got in the car and hurried to find the place where the drone had taken off.

"Who do you think wrote the 'HELP!' message, Dad?" said Megan, on the way. "Do you think it was Shivam?"

"It looks that way!" said Dad.

When they came to the old bridge, Dad, Megan and Billy went over it. They followed the river – back the way that the drone had come from.

Bess jumped in the river.

"Bess!" said Megan. "That's not funny!" But Dad and Billy laughed.

Before long, they were near the Potts' farm.

Dad looked at the map on his phone again. "The first place we saw on the drone movie should be just over there," he said. "It's called 'Three Ways'. Come on!"

They got to Three Ways, and
looked all around.

"Shivam must be somewhere near,"
said Billy.

"But where?" said Megan.

Bess ran up to Dad. She looked up at him.

"What is it, old girl?" said Dad.

Bess barked at Dad – then suddenly ran off.

"Come on, you two!" said Dad. "After her!"

Bess ran on, into some trees. Dad, Billy and Megan followed her.

"Shivam!" said Billy. "We found you!"

"Good girl, Bess!" said Megan.

Their friend looked down at them from high up in a tree. He looked very pleased to see them!

"I'm stuck!" he said. "Can you help me, please?"

It did not take long for Dad to help Shivam climb down from the tree.

"I took my new drone out for the first time," said Shivam. "But it got stuck in the tree. I climbed up to get it. Then I couldn't get down again."

"So you wrote a message on your drone . . ." said Megan.

". . . And made it fly off to get help!" said Billy. "That was clever thinking!"

"Good thing you had a pen in your pocket," said Dad.

"I've got loads of things in my pockets!" said Shivam.

Bess barked at Dad.

Dad laughed. "Yes, old girl – I know you found him!" he said. "Cameras and phones and laptops are all very clever, but not half as clever as you!"

As Bess barked again, Megan, Billy and Shivam all laughed, too.

How much do you remember about the story of The Mystery Drone? Answer these questions and find out!

- Who finds the drone?

- What message is written on the drone?

- How do Megan and Billy find out where the drone came from?

- What is the name of the farm they look for?

- Where do they find Shivam?

Look at the different story sentences and match them to the characters who said them.

"There's something written on it. It's a message!"

"When you fly a drone like this one, its camera takes a movie."

"I'll get my laptop."

"I've got loads of things in my pockets!"

www.ladybird.com